I have something to protect right here. I won't forget that.
I'll never forget this warmth, this heartbeat.

Melanie Shoen
Translation

Miss V
Retouch and Lettering

Topaz Bailey
Designer

Michelle Locque
Director of Print Production

Mariko Kumanoya
Publisher

Kizuna: Bonds of Love - Book 4. Published by Be Beautiful™, an imprint of A18 Corporation. Office of Publication – 250 West 57th Street, Suite 328, New York, NY 10107. Original Japanese version "Kizuna Vol. 4"

Price per copy $15.99, price in Canada may vary.
ISBN: 1-933440-05-8. Catalog number: CMX 69704G.
UPC: 8-51988-00105-9-00411. Printed in Canada.

Kizuna 4

Bonds of Love

Story and Art by Kazuma Kodaka

Contents

Character Descriptions 6
Story So Far 10
Kizuna: Bonds of Love 13
Afterthoughts 197
About Kazuma Kodaka 199
Interview with Kazuma Kodaka 200

Character Profiles

Kei Enjyoji

Tall, dark, and handsome, and the intended target of the hit and run driver that almost killed Ranmaru. Overcome with guilt, Kei has tried to make amends to his lover ever since that fateful day, including helping Ranmaru with his painful physical therapy. An outcast from his own family because he is the illegitimate son of his yakuza father's mistress, Kei has a half-brother named Kai who shows up from time to time, usually making things worse for our heroes.

Skill set: Studious, passionate, fashion conscious

Ranmaru Samejima

This former kendo star must learn to cope with the nagging injuries to his right arm that have ended his athletic career. Finds himself in a prolonged and passionate relationship with Kei Enjyoji, the son of a yakuza boss. He has found a degree of peace since settling down with Kei, although his past as a kendo champion threatens to haunt him for the rest of his days.

Skill set: Kendo, well-developed sense of introspection, a good kisser

Kai Sagano

Kei's half-brother enjoyed the advantages of being raised in a yakuza family. Grew up to be relatively fearless, mainly due to the constant presence of his bodyguard, Masa, for whom he has developed rather amorous feelings. Took up kendo as a way to meet Ranmaru, but was unable to strike up a romantic relationship with the kendo champ. Years later, when he was reunited with his half-brother, Kai was ecstatic at this new opportunity to get close to Ranmaru. Will he be the wedge that drives Ranmaru and Kei apart?

Skill set: Kendo, cooking, getting into trouble with both sides of the law

Masanori (Masa) Araki

This well muscled soldier in the Sagano yakuza family has been Kai's personal bodyguard for many years. His relationship with Kai works on many levels, including a not too subtle sexual tension that each of them would love to further explore. His deep affection for Kai is mirrored by his crueler side, that of the Sagano family's enforcer, a leg-breaking killer who can be ruthless and calculating.

Skill set: Proficient with edged weapons, all manner of larceny, and general treachery

Story So Far

RANMARU SAMEJIMA and KEI ENJYOJI met in college. They were inseparable, getting in trouble together and studying together, and then the inevitable happened, and the smoldering sparks between them ignited into full born flames of passion!

Ranmaru was a kendo star, while Kei was the black sheep of his family, the yakuza Sagano clan, as the illegitimate son of his father's mistress. But they overcame their differences and fell in love. However, all of that was about to change. During a clandestine check on Kei for his Sagano bosses, the hugely muscled MASANORI ARAKI brought along a guest to Ranmaru's kendo tournament...Kei's half-brother, KAI SAGANO, who was instantly enamored with the fiery kendo champion.

Upon his return to headquarters, Masanori learned of a power struggle within the underworld. The ailing head of the Sagano family wanted Masanori to take the reins of the power, but his loyalty to the Sagano bloodline wouldn't allow him to do so. Word that a Sagano heir must assume control spread throughout the underworld, which resulted in an attempt on Kei's life...an assassination attempt by car! The would-be killer missed Kei, but gravely injured Ranmaru.

When Kai heard of this, he tried to see Ranmaru, but Masanori wouldn't allow it and forcibly restrained him until the danger was over, which would only be when a new leader of the Sagano clan had been named.

Against all odds, Kei and Ranmaru continued their college careers, and engaged in a series of romantic misadventures.

Again, their happiness was not to last, when Kai returned, holding a grudge against Kei because he wanted Ranmaru's love for himself.

Eventually, Kai finally seduced Ranmaru for an evening to remember...

Afterwards, Ranmaru confessed his infidelity, and he and Kei shared a passionate lovemaking session.

The next morning, our three heroes forged an uneasy alliance. Kai was summoned to return home by Masanori, and our lovers were happy to have their privacy again. What will become of our heroes? Only time will tell...

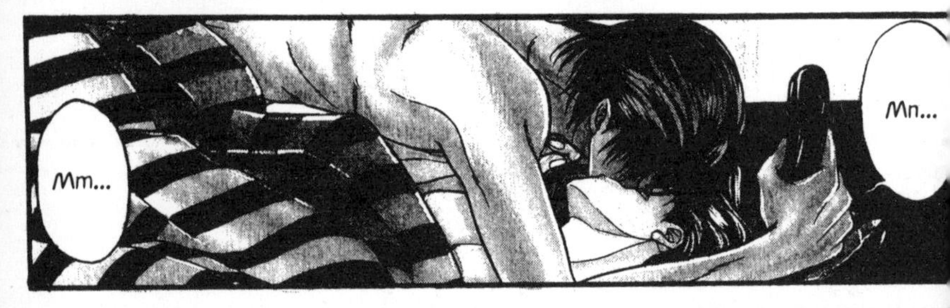

Cut it out, lover. Let me sleep a while longer...

Your grandpa's on the phone.

You should have said so!!

Oww.

KIZUNA

ZUNA

絆
きずな

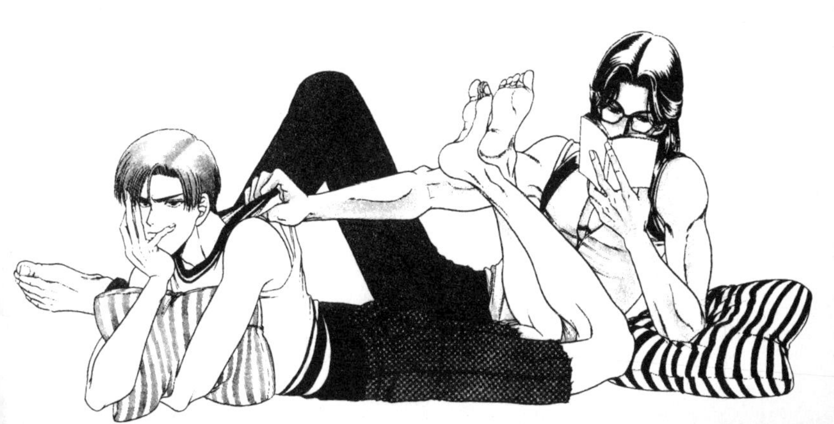

Hello?
Sleeping through the afternoon? What a lazy life you lead, **Ranmaru.**
No, Grandpa. Not at all! I was up late last night...uhhh, ***studying!***
Ah! So you're busy with college?

In any case, you've been in the neighborhood all this time and we haven't seen you.
Yes, Grandpa. I'm ***sorry,*** Grandpa.
Is there some reason you can't visit? I'm sure there isn't.
Um, well...
Uh-oh...

Sounds like I'm in for a **lecture** today.
Um, yes, you're right.
Wah!
FWOOSH

What are you **thinking!?** I'm on the phone!

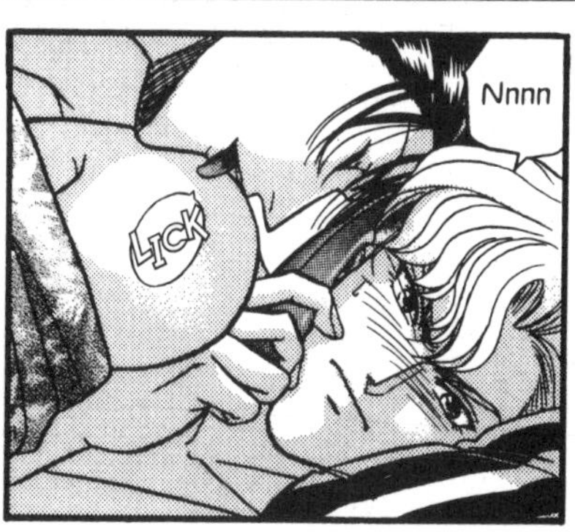

Oh it's nothing, Grandpa. **Really.**

Well you...you see, I've been kinda... **busy.**

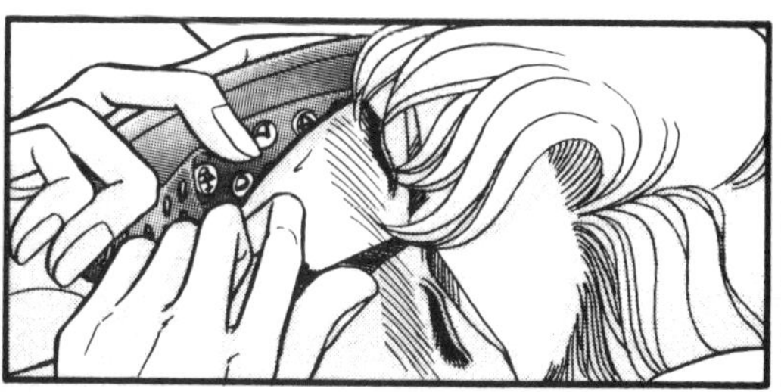

Nnnn...

I...

I under-stand. I'll come today!
Excuse me.

CLICK

"I'll come **today!?**" You're going **home!?**
......
We were going out today! You **promised!**

What gives? This isn't a formal marriage interview, is it?

And whose fault is **that**, huh?
GRIND GRIND
Ow ow ow
I couldn't refuse because ***you*** were distracting me!

Don't forget that I'm the **Samejima Family** heir.

Maybe.
HMPH
Hey, no way!!

I've left the dojo in someone else's hands just to be here.
Anything that goes wrong during my absence will be ***my*** fault.
So I'll go today. It's just ***one*** day. That's all.

I'll get it over with quickly. I'll be back **tonight.**
Hey.
?
What?
Will you be okay all by yourself?
I can come with...
Don't worry.
I'll be fine.

Enjyoji's offer was heartfelt, but I really couldn't accept it.

If this had anything to do with him, I would've been glad to have him along.

But this is *my* problem.

It's difficult... standing before these gates... now that I've given up Kendo.

But thoughts like that won't get me anywhere.
Here I go!
CREAK
*Samejima
Keep going!!
WHACK
FLINCH
Eyaaah!!
WHACK
WHACK
WHACK
WHACK

Louder! I can't hear you!!

Attack your opponent with voice and spirit!!
Bring your voice from the depths of your gut!!

WHACK
WHACK
Eyaaaah!!
Daahh

CLENCH
The rough sound of a bamboo sword.

The atmosphere of warm spirit...

It's so nostalgic.

Mr. Same-jima!?
は
HUH?

How are you!? When did you arrive?
I'm sorry, **Master Kureba-yashi.** I didn't mean to interrupt...
No, not at all.
CLUNK
CLUNK

I didn't know you were coming today. Please come in.
Ah, yes. How to say this?

I'm... not doing Kendo anymore.
Then you can just watch, if you'd like.
We must keep an eye on the beginners.
SMILE
Of course.
That's a **guy**... right?
ほけー… STARE
Who is it?
Dunno ...

This is the **Master's grandson**!

He's here to make **sure** you don't **slack off**!!

Hey! Stop blabbering!

...Or something like that, huh?

Sure.

Begin !!

Ahh...I knew it.

暮林

Kurebayashi↗

WHACK

Daaaah!

Eyaaaah!

HACK

*This is where it all began. Where **I** began.*

*Being here is **already** making me tense.*

I **thought** you might be here.

Oh! Forgive me...

So, you don't tell your Grandfather that you've **arrived?**

Hmph.
どかっ
THUMP
BOW
Please excuse me! I've arrived, sir!

Somehow, we've managed to get along **without** you.
Hmph.
Forgive me for not visiting for so **very** long.

Your hands...
Excuse me?
Aren't your hands **itching** by now?

You don't look like you're ***satisfied*** with just watching.
After all...
I'm the one who raised you that way.

Come with me.
We will eat. And talk.
Yes.
!!

We've gotten a few more pictures since your last visit.
There should be one of **Shizuho** here, somewhere.
Really?

That picture was taken just after the tournament. You **should** remember.

Where?
All the way in the back.

*A **great** fighter, who gave **every-thing** to Kendo.*
*The woman they called the **White Faced Ogre.***

*Yes...I **do** remember.*

Mother.

But to me, her hand was always kind and warm.

Oh my! It's Master Ranmaru!

I heard we had a guest coming, but I had no idea it was you!

Hello, Miyo. How you doing?

I've been well, but you've gotten all skinny again!?
Yes, well...It's been such a long time...
Yes, yes, it has! Now that the Miss has married off, my master's been so lonely!

Miyo.
You had that Funawa sweet potato paste, didn't you?
COUGH
I'm so sorry, but you ate every last bit of it yesterday, Sir.
If I'd known the young master was coming, I would've said something.
I'll go buy some more.
No need to trouble yourself!

Ah, yes.
Your tea is getting cold.

It's my pleasure, so please relax.
Please, Miyo... don't!

I haven't had any... **particular** trouble.
How have you been faring?

.....

Have you tried weilding a bamboo sword?

Yes?
...Ran-maru.

No.

I...no longer...
Ranmaru.

I'm not asking you to **fight.** I'm only listening to your honest heart.
I won't say everything **can** be as before, but if you come back I can help you.

The spot for **senior instructor** is open.
Then Master Kurebayashi should be the one to...
Kurebayashi wanted to give **you** the right of first refusal.
But Grandfather, **you** should know better than I...
...How can someone who once gave up Kendo **possibly** be a teacher!?

CLENCH
I'm just saying that path is still **open** to you.

And to be honest, I don't wish to **repeat** the mistakes I made with Shizuho.
AH...
はっ…

Choose what you think is best.
*Can I really **live** for Kendo...*

*...Like my mother, who lost my father's **love**...and then her **life?***

Can I accept those things along with her memory?

Grand-father...

I need a little time...to ***think*** about it.

I usually wouldn't do this, but with **Rikako** away, I guess I'll tag along.
I don't wanna go on a date with **you.**
I got it.

I guess I can deal with this since you're ***treating*** me.
TCHH
I'm ***not*** treating you.
You're paying for yourself.

That's not fair! You told me you had an extra ticket!!
I do.
And it'll cost you 1400 yen* --pretty cheap.
Hey!
*About $13.30
Just seeing you pisses me off.
The feeling is mutual.

You know him?
My brother. Kai.
Really? You don't look alike.

We have different mothers.
Oh, sorry.
It's all right.

I don't like to think that he's even half related to me.
Oh, really...?
Still your same bratty self, I see.

I don't take that kinda talk from anyone!
Oh yeah? I'll shut you up, wait and see.
TUG
I think I'll be going, Enjyoji.

1400 yen.
You get obnoxious when money's involved.

I'm telling on you.
Why?
You're cheating on him.
Don't be stupid.

By the way...how **is** he?

Why do you **care?**
I don't. I've got nothing else to ask.

He's fine. Okay? Just **fine.**

Okay.

Are you...**sick** or something?
None of your business.

Ahh, I see how it is.

You're homesick.
Shut up! I am **not**!
Well, if you don't have a home, at **least** you've got **Araki**.

!!
You were talking in your sleep during your last visit.
BLUSH
Saying *"Ohhh, Masa..."*

Whoa.
FWACK

GRAB

If you have time to hit me...

...Don't you have time to **call him?**

There there

Shut up!!

Let go, you moron!!

Don't act like my brother... we're **hardly** even related!

You're **nothing** as far as I'm concerned!

Kom

Still bratty. And **loud.**
魚善
ミラノ
シネミ

I'm home.

Welcome back.

Are you working tonight?
Yeah, I'm just heading out.
What about dinner?
Already ate. Sorry.

Enjyoji?
Yes?

.....
What?

Nothing. I'll tell you later.

All right.

No solitary **brooding**, okay?
Okay.

CLICK

I can't go **halfway.**
Master Kurebayashi is only looking out for me because of my past accomplishments.

B-TAK
After the accident, I was told my right side would never move again. But I didn't suffer through my rehabilitation for the sake of my Kendo.
It was for Kei...because I didn't want to be a burden to him. I've worked hard since then so we could always be equals.
But now...I'm wavering.
It's not fair of me to want Kei to tell me not to go back to it.

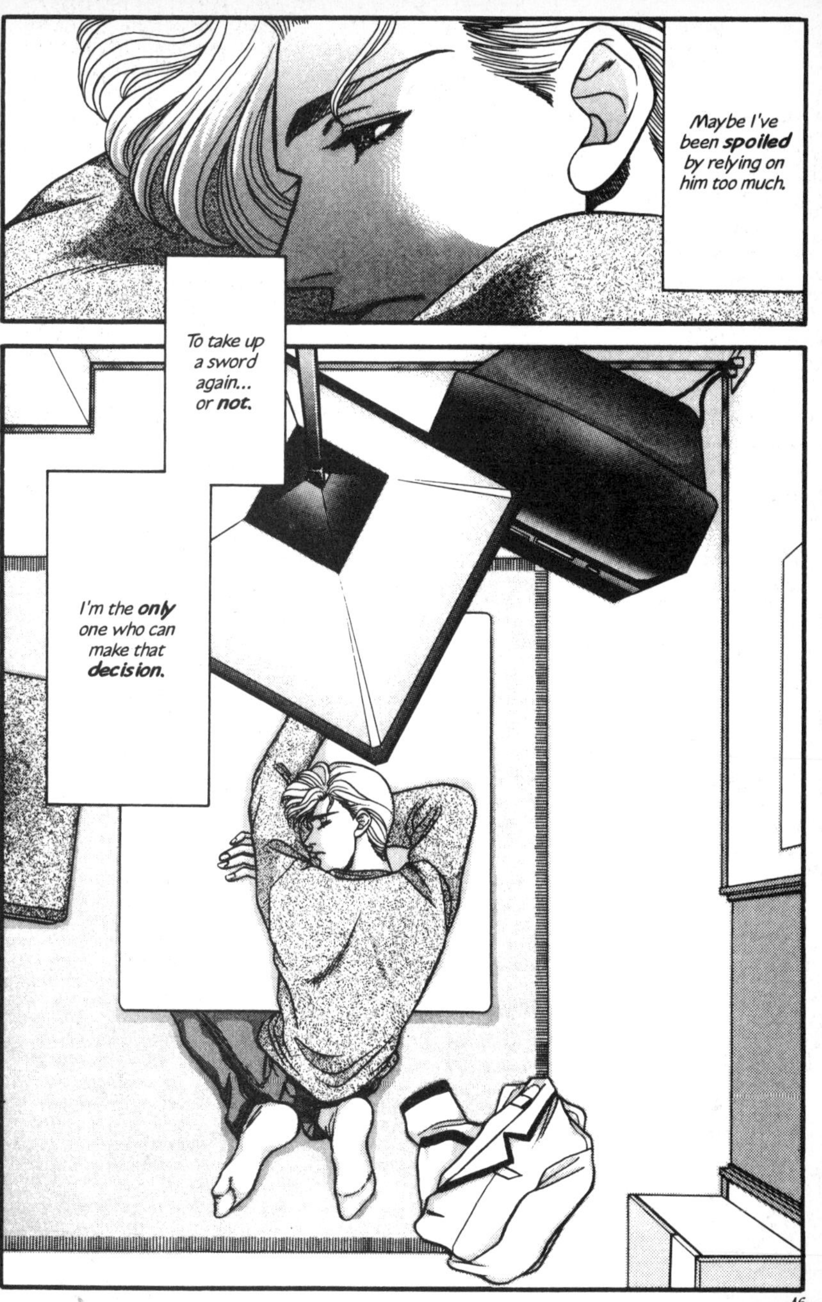
Maybe I've been **spoiled** by relying on him too much.
To take up a sword again... or **not**.
I'm the **only** one who can make that **decision**.

G-CHAN
THUMP

RING RING
This is **Kai Sagano.**

Young sir? It's **been** a while. This is **Toshi.**
The boss? Funny you should ask.
He's with his advisor in Tokyo right now.

Kyosuke's with him?
Damn, I forgot! He's **also** in Tokyo, isn't he?
Yes.

I didn't know about that.
Well, it was all very sudden.
Should I contact them for you?

CLICK
NO!!

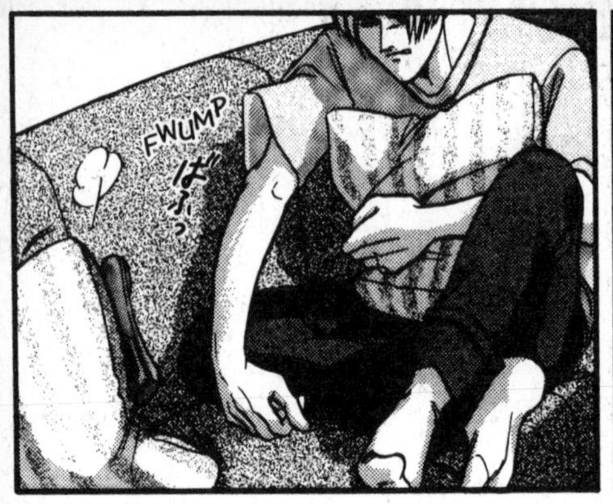
FWUMP
ばふっ

They're here in Tokyo and I don't even get a call?

I haven't seen him in three ***months***!
How I long to hear your voice, Masa.

歌舞伎町一番街

When will I see you again?

Soon. I wouldn't want you to **forget** me.

Are you testing my endurance?
Possibly. Be good until we meet again.

Thank you very much!
VROOM

Cat's

I'm tired.

That **idiot.**

Go ahead without me.
PMPH
Why?

Kei! Where are you going?
I'll be back!

Hey! Watch it!
Sorry, miss.

What are you doing here?

!!
BEEP BEEP
SCREECH

You idiot!
You're the one that's speeding!!
HAAH HAAH
はー はー
VRRRRM
リス
フェレンギ

Kai?
TURN

Damn.

!

Where'd he get off to?

Why am I looking after Kai, anyway?
He makes me so mad.

He'd better not be doing something **dangerous** again.
FSSH

What does the Ozu family want, anyway?

Recently, the leaders of **Shohokai** from the Kanto region met with the **Shoryukai** from Kansai.

I must know...Did something **happen** with the Ozu then?

No.

The man we're going to meet, **Sasazuka,** isn't well liked among the Ozu directors.

Well, the Ozu **did** call for us, even if it isn't a big deal.

Well, Imagawa, that's because they want to see if our **new** boss has given us **new leadership.**
They've summoned us tonight just to **tease** us.

Everyone is divided by **age.** It provides ***some*** respite from the fools.

We can avoid outright fighting because we don't have so many **hot-heads.**

Ha ha! Well said
It's always the **juniors** th come out shooting.

.....

Boss?
Hm?
Is this all right?

You haven't called him.

We came all this way and didn't contact him once.
Won't this **anger** him?

That cute little mouth of his is gonna **pout.**
For **sure.**

Sigh... You're right.

I'll contact him later... when things calm down.
*Has it **really** been three months since I've heard his voice?*

カツ TAK
カツ TAK
カツ TAK

キイ!! SCREECH

You're **Mr. Araki,** the young boss from Shoryukai's Sagano Clan?
This way, please.

Mr. Araki!
You finally made it!

Come, sit down! Ladies, will you excuse us? I'll call for you later.
Yes, sir.
Excuse us.

My apologies for being late, Mr. Sasazuka. I am Araki, the representative from the Sagano family. This is my advisor, **Imagawa.**

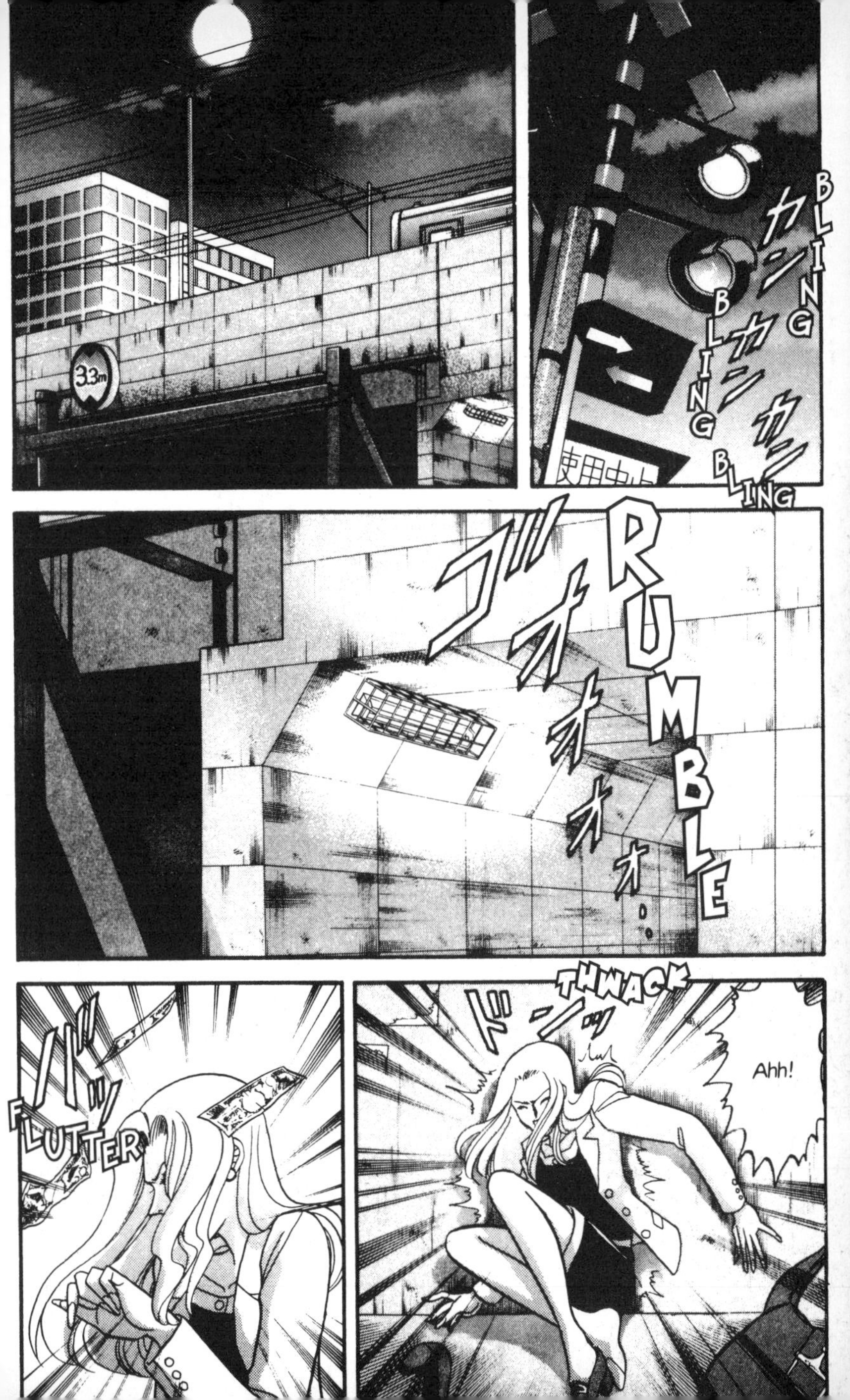
カーンカーンカーン
BLING
BLING
BLING
ブオオオオオ…
RUMBLE
バババ
FLUTTER
ドーンッ
THWACK
Ahh!

I don't get you, lady.
My... money...

That isn't enough.
You're lying!

Ask that guy! He told me 30,000 yen* would be enough, like last time!
*About $285

Really? He told me it's not enough.

Sagano here is the son of the Sagano Family of the Kansai yakuza.
You don't want something bad to happen when you don't pay up, do you?

Pleased to meet you. I am Imagawa, advisor to the Sagano Family's representative.

Spare me your awkward greetings.

GLARE

Very well.

In **that** case...

Sit down and be silent.

Our group assembly is coming up.
Tell me... How's your boss?
He's doing well, thank you.
Is he, now? That's **good** to hear.

What effects Shoryukai affects Shohokai.

Not to mention the Sagano Clan and the Ozu.
LIFT

Japan's yakuza consists of these two prominent families.
CLINK
Yes.
Thank you.

Thank you.
Hmph.

Here we drink our *saké* from different glasses.
But we **never** drink from each other's glass.
We live by **imbibing** the contents from our **own** glass.

If a drop should spill, that constitutes a **break** in the rules.
It's up to the one who has spilled it to clean up their mess.

Tell me.
Have there been drops spilling from ***your*** glass?

What's he trying to say with this roundabout speech?

That's a pretty metaphor. But if you're trying to ***apply*** that to the Sagano Family...

...That's not something my ***superior*** would pay any mind to.

Would you please get to the ***point***, sir?

Getting right to the point, I see. I ***like*** that.

Well then, there seems to be some confusion among our junior members.

In the midst of a routine operation, they somehow obtained a large quantity of illegal drugs.

As you know, dealing in drugs is ***forbidden*** for us.

Although ***experienced*** men like ***ourselves*** would know better, ***they*** went through with it.

You see, it's simply not good business. We yakuza have great **pride** in our fighting strength.
If this unfortunate indiscretion catches the eye of the police, our reputation would be **tarnished.**
The proof has been disposed of. The men dealt with.

The Ozu Family does not like **loose ends**, and so those men have been retired.

How-ever...

In the process of "dealing with" them, one of them blurted out something strange.

He claimed the **Sagano** Family was behind it.
What are you saying!? Where's the proof...!?
CLATTER
Kyosuke!

The seller was actually a smaller clan called Tsuneya.
Curiously, we didn't find the name anywhere in our investigation.
There isn't any proof.
I... excuse me.

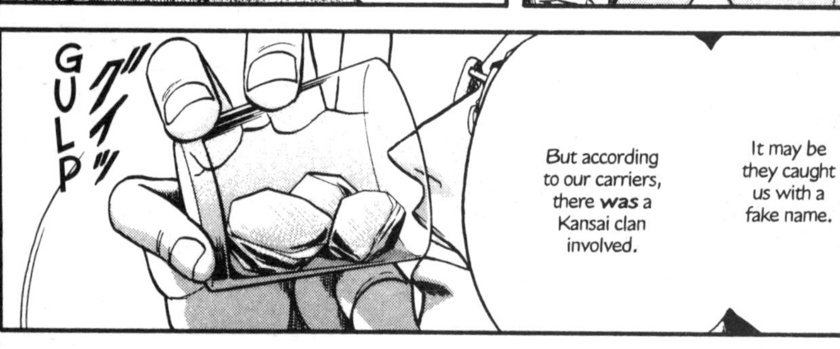
GULP
It may be they caught us with a fake name.
But according to our carriers, there was a Kansai clan involved.

And Kansai is Shoryukai's "island." We can't do much on our own over there.
On the other hand, we don't want an all-out war between east and west, either.
CLUNK

We understand. The Sagano Family will take over the investigation.
STAND

As the Sagano name has been compromised, I'd **appreciate** your **discretion** until we've completed our work.

FWOOP
Dammit! He pisses me off!!

How could you look so damn calm while he throws everything on **us**!?
Calm down, Kyosuke.

He's been unable to settle this mess, and when a **war** breaks out he'll make it look like **our** faults!!

It's not that big of a deal. He's just thinking of expanding his "island."

Perhaps we should try and find the guys who were "retired" a while back?
Think we can? They've probably all gone ***straight*** by now.
Not **all** of them. They're using the Sagano name, after all.

Maybe this is all just a misunder-standing.
Maybe.

Kai needs a bodyguard.
Ah!

Should I stay here?
No. I'll need you with me.

Then we have to call Toshi.
No, wait.

I have an idea.

There's **one** man I haven't seen in several years, but he'd do.
He **was** a professional bodyguard, wasn't he?
Yeah.

But his specialty wasn't **protecting**...

...It was **house-work.**

Merely a **euphemism** for a professional assassin.

ESSO

オイルスピード交

Thank you very much!

Hey Tashiro, you have a call!
Okay, thanks!
バッテリー

Hello?

It's Araki.

It's been a few years.

I want to talk about a job. Can I meet you?

I don't **usually** meet with my clients...
...But you've always been **special**.

When? **That** soon? Okay.
TAP TAP
パタ パタ
You're in Tokyo?

Yes, but I'm leaving the hotel tomorrow. Can you meet me here?

Sure, but you won't recognize me. My face has **changed** since last time.

I don't care about your face. Just come.
Hmmm. **Tough** guy.

I'll be right over. Who knows? Maybe we'll get it on.
Heh heh
No chance. This is ***strictly*** business.

Hey Boss... he's still an assassin, right?

If anyone's after Kai, he'll get them **first.**

Besides, we can't track Kai using **known** yakuza. It'd only make him look **bad.**

Tashiro's good. And if it comes down to it, he's got the guts to take a **hit** for Kai.
Oh, one other thing: Take off before he gets here. He won't meet with anyone else.

Hey Boss, are you **into** this guy or something ?
You seem to know all of his quirks.
WHACK

.....
STING じんじん
Just don't get in too deep.
Otherwise, it'll be trouble all over again.

Good work today!

What, leaving already?
So sorry. I have **obligations** to which I must attend.
So you say. Are you **sure** it's not a woman?

Very sure. Good night.
Heh. See ya.

Excuse me.
Mr. Enjyoji, isn't it?

Police Department
Do you have a minute?
I'm sorry...
...Have I done something to trouble the police?
If not, then g bother someon else.
Kai Sagano.
He's your half-brother, isn't he, Mr. Enjyoji?

So **that's** it.
All right, then. Speak your piece, and I'll pass it along to his guardian.
That's all I can do for you.
KCHH
So?
What did he do **this** time?
COFFEE
珈琲

You get straight to the point, don't you?

There's no point doing otherwise.

Sagano **is** a yakuza family, after all.

I'm sure they do **plenty** to bother the police.
Besides, if you **did** suspect Kai of some crime, you'd just arrest him.

Am I right?

It'd be nice if we could.

I may be related to the Sagano by blood, but I **don't** want anything to do with them.

Yes, so you say.

But back to your brother...

Did you know that he's suspected of distributing illegal narcotics?

Your brother's name came up **repeatedly** during the interrogation of several suspects.

We suspect Kai is intimately involved, organizing meeting places and gathering buyers.

Our investigation has been hampered because his organization does their best to impede our work.

So you're planning a **decoy** operation?
What if you don't get the **proof** you need?

Why don't you just arrest him?
Because we don't **only** want him. We want the entire organization, trade route and all.

You'll just expose your men to unnecessary **danger.**

Hmph.

Please **cooperate** with us, Mr. Enjyoji. We can **guarantee** your brother will be treated fairly.
After all, we understand **why** you hate the police...
What do you mean?

I'm referring to the **hit-and-run** incident that injured your friend, of course.
FLINCH

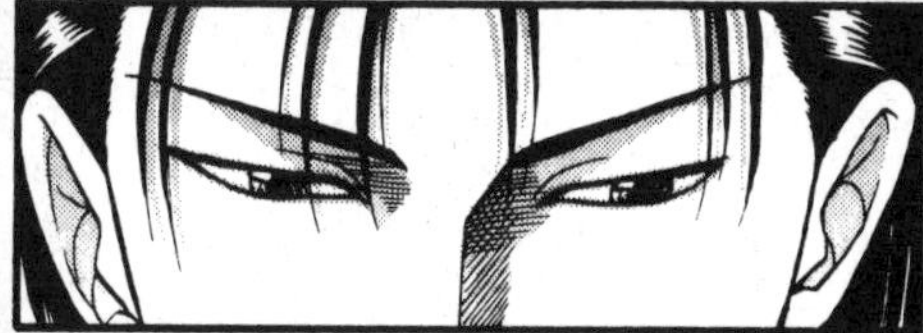

Coincidentally, my colleague was in charge of that case.

Your friend... Samejima ...
...you two were **close,** weren't you?

CLENCH
Did you know, Mr. Enjoyoji, that the driver was aiming for ***you...***

GRIP
...But he missed, and hit Samejima instead.

I'm sure you were angry enough to have made war with the Sagano all by yourself.
But the Sagano are too powerful. And you are just **one man.** And looking into you further...

...You probably lacked the courage to go **against** them.

So I ask you again, Mr. Enjyoji. Please cooperate with us...

...So that painful incidents like that won't happen to others.

Bastard. You have a lot of nerve, digging up my past like that.
Am **I** a suspect, too?
Not at all.
I didn't mean it like that.

You know, if the police were able to arrest him then, that would have changed my mind a little bit...

I was told the law would punish the man, so I cooperated.
But instead, he turned up dead.
And it was really not ***satisfying*** that way.

It's not that I'm **protecting** Kai.
I just don't trust that the police will be able to bring the guys as far as a courtroom.

That's all I have to say.

Thanks for the coffee.

Can I ask you one more thing?

Did you see your brother this afternoon?

I did.

Around one o'clock. We saw a movie in Shinjuku.

Okay?

...You gonna
investigate
that?

I still have
the stub...

No,
thank
you.
Thanks
for talking
with us.

ELEX
3F

You **sure** you wanna let him go?
It's fine.

He's got **good eyes.**
Huh?

There's something **important** that he's protecting.
Enough to threaten the police with his eyes.

Threaten with his **eyes?**
The bastard's got guts.
Don't worry about it.

I'm home--huh!?

Hey! Why are you sleeping **here?**

You're going to catch a cold like that!
Mm...
You're home early.

I was just taking a nap...
Look this way! Do you have a fever!?
What's with ***you?***
I'm just worried. Hmm, can't tell.

Where's the damn thermometer?
You're over-reacting.
Just open your mouth.
Maybe you should check **yourself.**
Huh?
You're acting strange.
Maybe **you** have a fever.
I...I'm sorry. I'm always overreacting, aren't I?
Gotta stay calm.
At least it doesn't seem like you've been drinking.

!

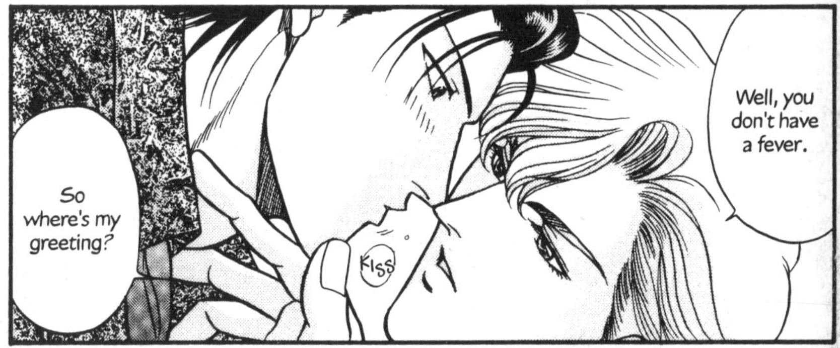
Well, you don't have a fever.
KISS
So where's my greeting?

"Hi, honey. I'm home."
That's more like it.
Now kiss me again.
Just a kiss?
Don't play games with me.

WHAP
Mm!
Mmmm!
Nnn?
Nn...
Nn...

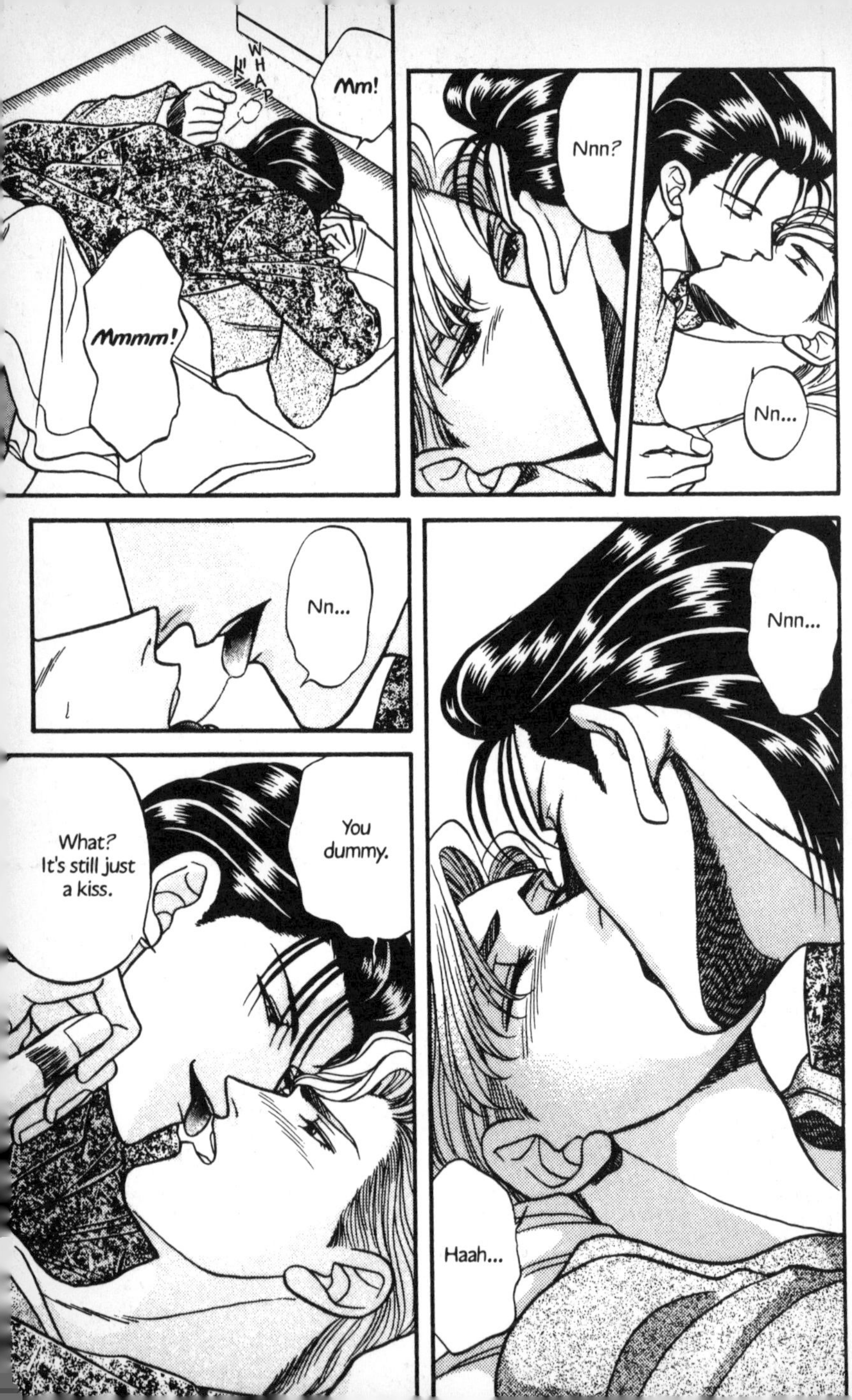

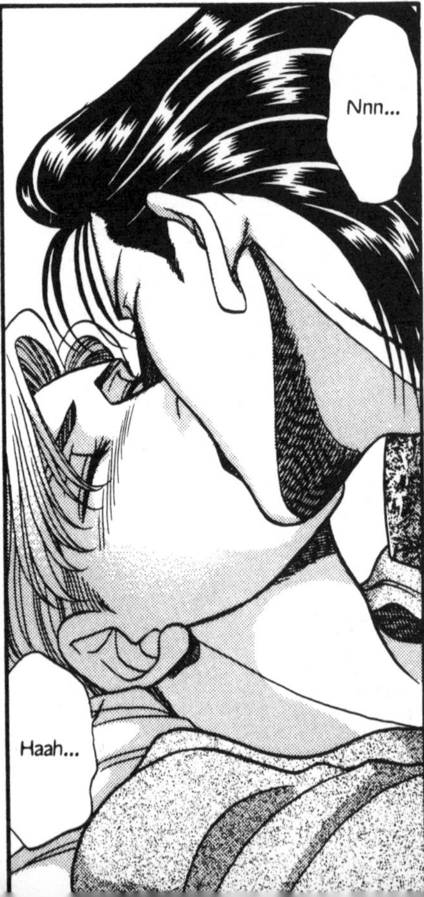

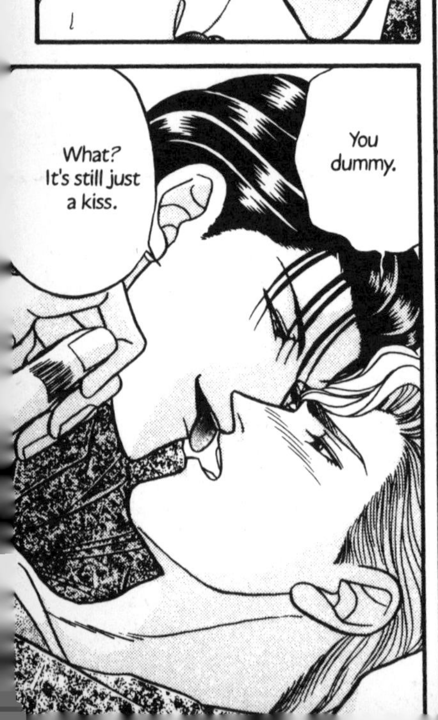

What? It's still just a kiss.
You dummy.

SLUMP
Can I stay here for a while?

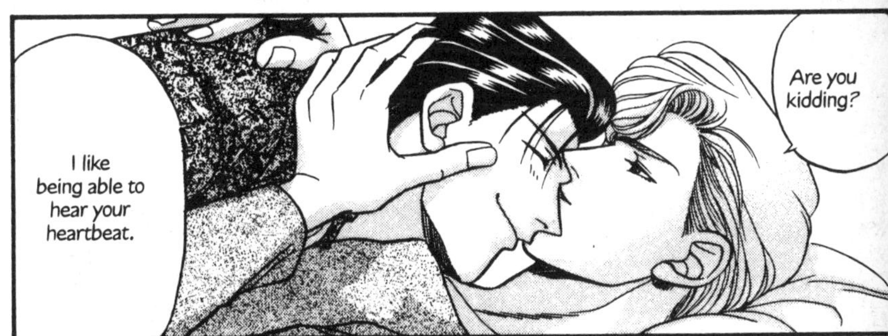
Are you kidding?
I like being able to hear your heartbeat.

I want to hear you.

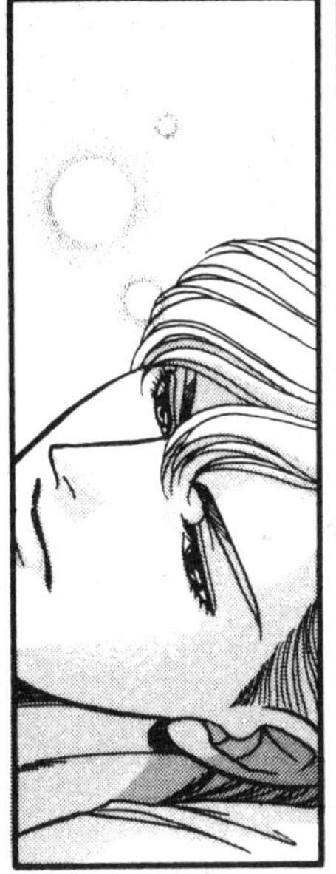

Okay...

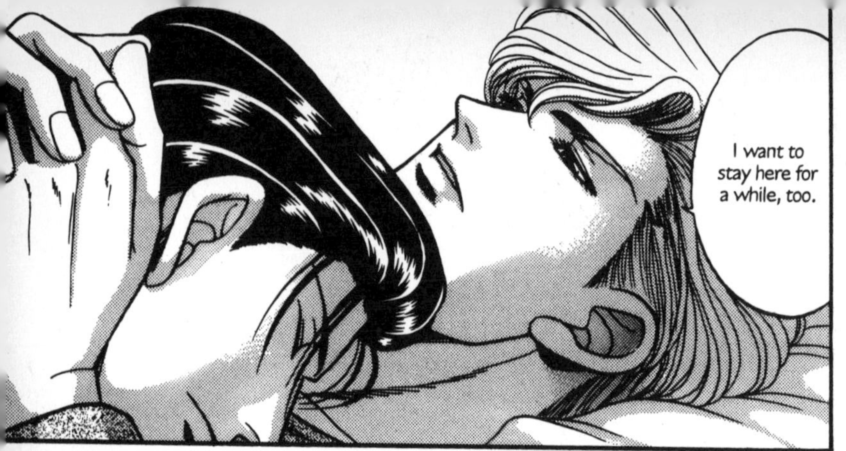

I have something to protect right here. I won't forget that.

I'll never forget this warmth, this heartbeat.

KCHA
シャラッ
JIGGLE
STEP
Some son of a yakuza *you* are.

You thought you could scare me because I'm a woman?
I'm not scared of **you.**
STEP
.....
Are you here to **kill** me? Is **that** it?

Shut up, you lousy crook!
I tried to pay back my debt to that gang...But **you** raised the price!

Give me that knife or you're going to get hurt.
STARE
I won't ask you **again.**

Mind your own business, creep!
Wha!?

Hey you guys! Keep it down out here!
CREAK

ガチャン
SLAM
Huff...
That lady is **crazy**!
The police ...
I've gotta call the police!
ジャリ
SHIFT
Say your prayers, little yakuza...
SLASH
...Because tonight you will die!

......
RING RING
SLAM
RING RING
You won't get away with this.
SWING
SNATCH

I don't know what you're blabbering about!!

You're crazy-- snap out of it!!

!!

CHOMP

Oww!

FLIP

WHAM

TWITCH
ピクッ
What a lousy day.
Hey, lady. Are you okay?
...?

!!
Help... me...
I don't want...to die...
.....
Help me...

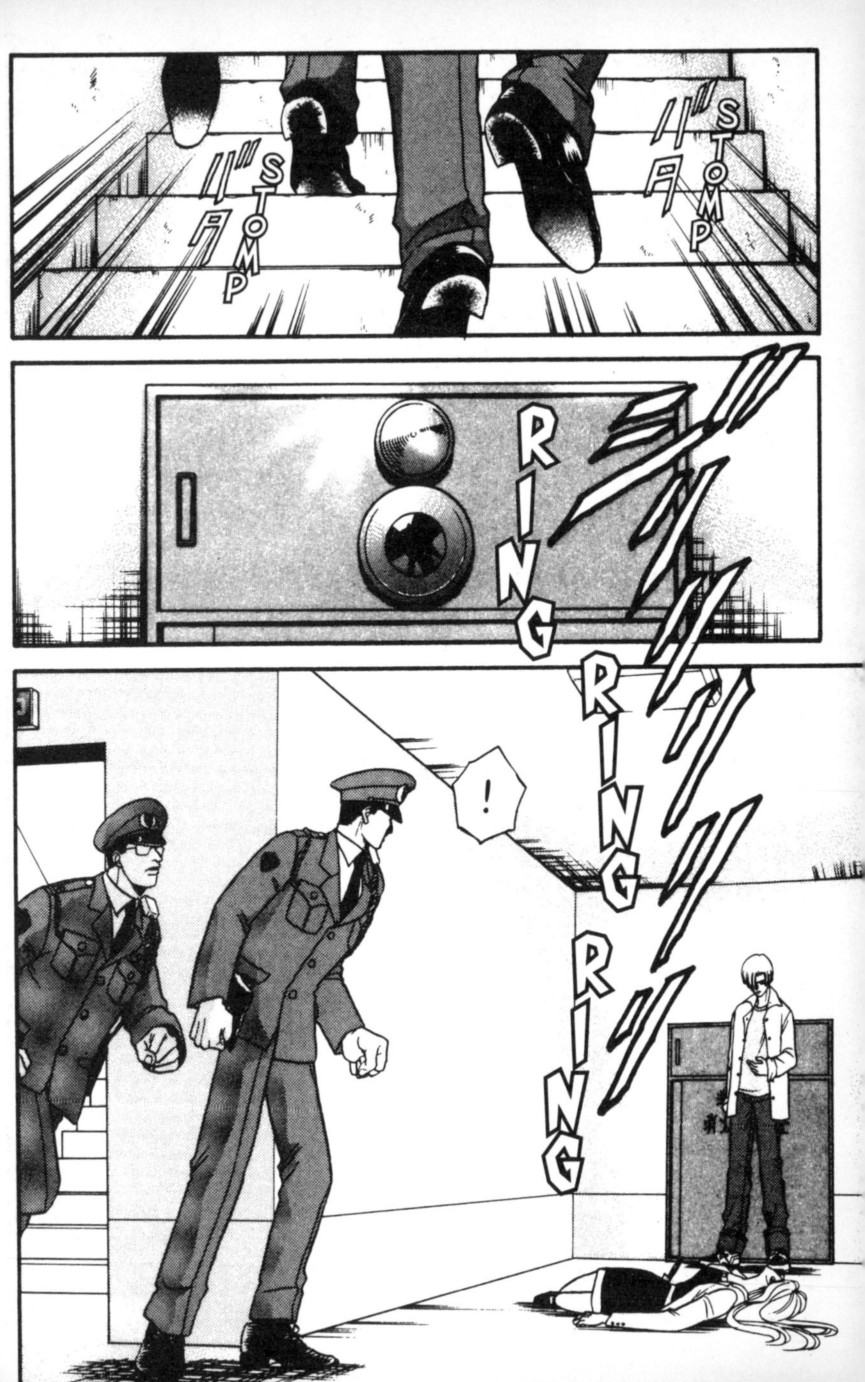
STOMP
STOMP
RING
RING
RING
!

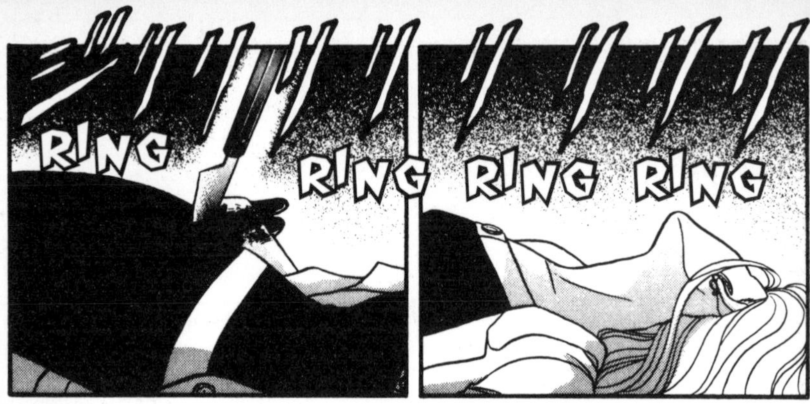

Hold on, miss. Help is on the way.

I **said** put your hands over your head!

I didn't do anything...

This isn't what it **looks** like!
It was...an **accident**!

As you know, bodyguard work isn't my specialty.
But I'll take the job.
I guess Little Mr. Sagano is important to your group.
But is he important to *you*?
So thanks for helping me. There's no one else I can ask.
WHIRL
Well, I guess no room for me to get between Araki and Kai.
I wonder why he wants me to guard this Kai? Well, I'll figure it out soon enough. ♡

Listen, punk. You're not making this any **easier** on yourself.
Why'd you stab that woman?!

I...
I didn't do **anything**.
RATTLE

You didn't, huh? So she stabbed **herself?**
SLAP
SLAM
CLATTER

Don't make too much of a mess of him. We'll get in trouble.

Nobody's gonna care about a punk like **him.** Guys like this just cause trouble for everyone.
ジャラ…
SLUMP

Hey, little yakuza.
I represent those little amateurs crying in your shadow.
KICK
ガッ

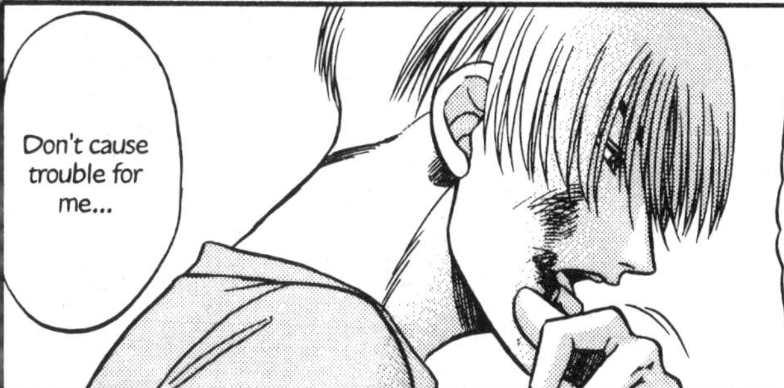
I'm making it my business to get every last one of you.
Don't cause trouble for me...

...You'll only come up short.
GRAB
Okay?
You may be high ranking to your criminal buddies, but to the **rest** of the world you're just **scum**!
I hope your daddy's proud of you.
.....
What did you say!?
WHAM
Guahh!

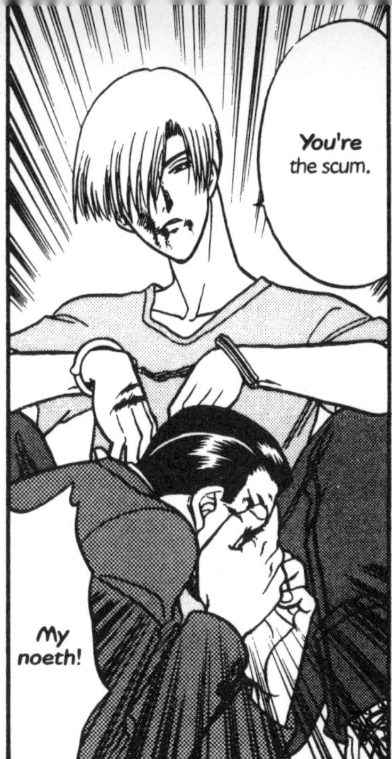
You're the scum.
My noeth!

GRAB
'E bwoke my noeth!

!
THUP
Never underestimate a yakuza, you idiot!
Nn--
SLUMP
Damn...

Talk. **Now.** Or else.
TSSHHH

TUG
Okay, you...
...This is your **last** chance.

Dabbit, I'll k'll 'im!!
Shut up...

I didn't **do** it!!

I...
Hm?

...You'll make my hand twitch. And we wouldn't want **that** to happen, **would** we?

GRIP
TAP

Ah!?
TWIST

You men are an **embarrassment.**
Ow ow ow! You don't understand!

Yes I **do.** And all too well.

Otsuki! Write down the details of his interrogation.
.....
Bud 'e bwoke muh **noeth**!

You idiot, I'll do far worse than **that**! Get **out** of here!
STARTLE
GULP

Uncuff him. Right away.
Yes... sir.

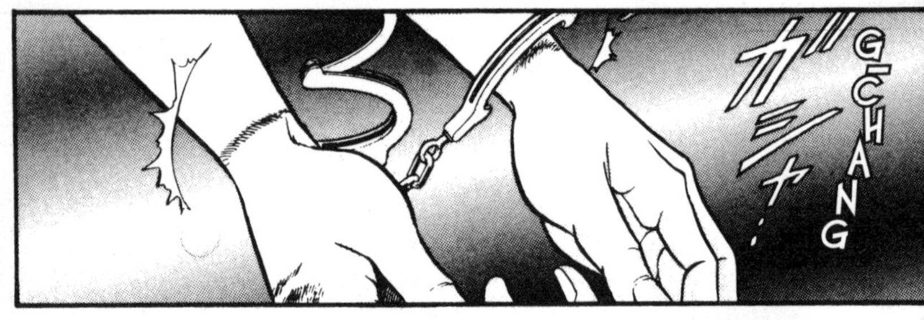
GCHANG

I'm sorry about this.
Damn fools!!

Are you all right, Mr. Sagano?
Do you need a doctor?
SETTLE

Would you like to have a seat?

.....

Sorry about those two brutes. You can sue them, if you want.
Hmph...
Yakuza suing the police? Don't make me laugh.

Your family may be yakuza, but are **you?**

You're not carrying drugs, not dealing, not hurting anyone...
In fact, you seem like a rather **average** citizen to me.

RATTLE

.....

Then why am I still here?

Okay. Will you listen to **my** side of the story?
Of **course.** Why do you think I'm sitting here? In fact, I even believe the stabbing was **accidental.**

I just wanted to look into your **eyes.**
My eyes?
Yes. When someone's committed a crime, you can **see it** in their eyes.

Your eyes aren't clouded by **guilt...**
...Although they **reak** of defiance.

I believe you're innocent.

Then I can go home?
Of course. Someone even came to get you.
Otsuki, go check on that for me.
All right.

Thank God... Masa came.
ほう SIGH

First Aid Room
Understood?
The investigation will be ongoing, so don't leave town.
ガチャ
G-CHAK
バタン…
SHUT
I feel awful.
I want to go home.
They really did you over.
Kai Sagano, right?

My name is Tashiro.
Nice to meet you.
WOBBLE きょろ
WOBBLE きょろ
.....
Araki isn't coming.
!?
It's just me.

Hey, hold up!

Araki hired me to look after you.

I'm not suppos-ed to leave your side!

Hey, are you listening?
WHIRL
Shut up! Don't follow me!!
STOMP
STOMP
I have to-- I'm your **bodyguard.**

Body-guard?
Yeah. Someone on the inside is **after** you, and I'm here to **protect** you.

I don't **need** you! I can take care of **myself**!

Hey! Wait up!
Don't tell **me** what to do!

That *flake is a bodyguard!? Yeah,* ***right!***
Why the hell did Masa stick me with ***that*** *idiot?*

Sigh. I didn't want it to **come** to this.
BEEP
BEEP

Hey, this is Tashiro.
Talk to Kai for me, okay?
I'm seriously going to **kill you**!
Just take the phone, okay? It's **Araki.**
WHIRL

...Hello?
SIGH

.....

Good.
I'll be over there.

I'm sorry about this, Kai. But I had to return home suddenly.

Tashiro may be **strange**, but you can trust him with your life.
WHEW!
It's only temporary, so please do what Tashiro says.

.....

Kai?
No.

I can't. I **won't...**
You hardly ever call me at all.

And now it's for something like **this?**

How could you **do** this to me?!

No, Kai. Not even for an instant.

Have you... **forgotten** about me?

You **liar**! When have you **ever** thought about anything other than the Family?
And now...when I need you the most...you leave me with a total **stranger**! That isn't right!

Please, Kai...Just listen to Tashiro.
We'll talk again later.
BEEP
Huh!?
He hung up?

Ah, you're so mean, Araki.
.....
RING
RING

Come on.

It'll be okay. Just...give me back the phone.

DASH
Sheesh.

Hey, Kai! Come back!
Aw, dammit...

Ugh.
SCREECH

Kai, wait!!
WHIRL
SLAM
What a jerk.
SCREECH
VROOM
Well, he's not ditching me ***that*** easily.

You can't just run around by yourself.

Otherwise, I wouldn't be a very good bodyguard, eh?

GASP ゼーはー

!?

WORMING IN
Go away! I never agreed to this!
I know that, but it's my **job**, you know.
PULL

SWING
And I won't get **paid** if you're murdered.
Umph

STARE
As if I care! Leave me alone, you psycho!

Ah, hello! I heard you testified on Kai's behalf.
Thank you very much!

Uh, no problem ...

Well, Kai needs his rest. He's had a **rough** day, y'know.
All those cops and crazy women and all...
!

Anyway, sorry about the fuss.

G-CHAK

.....

First a knife-wielding woman, and now this guy. What's going on?

Hmm.

Everything's cluttered, but in neat little piles.

Did Araki rub off on you?

None of your business!

Don't touch anything!

The weather tomorrow will be sunny…
You finished talking to Araki, didn't you?
Main phone
Secondary phone

Huh?
No dial tone.

Cut it out! I **told** you not to touch anything!
GRAB
Can you please stop yelling for a while?

Ahh, so this **isn't** a first for you, **is** it? Look, if you'll just listen to me, you won't cause Araki any trouble. Okay?

Listen, Tashiro. I don't want you here. I don't **need** you here.
I'm only doing this for Araki, okay?

As if I care!

All he thinks about is the yakuza. He only cares about me as far as his **career** is concerned.

Hmm...

You might as well **accept** it until this is over.
After that, you can complain all you want.

I think that would be **best.**
Right?
I don't have to listen to **you.**
My **name** is Tashiro.

Nice to meet ya.
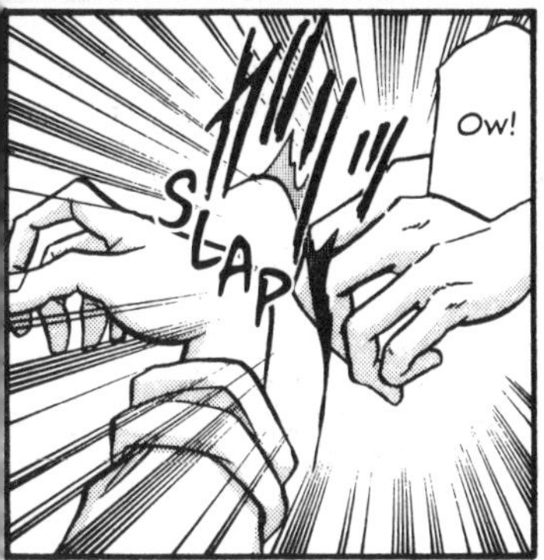
Ow!
SLAP

That hurt!

SLAM
He's like an angry cat.
SIGH

I'll need to be careful. Even a **tamed** cat still has claws.

All that Masa cares about is his precious yakuza. But what about **me?**

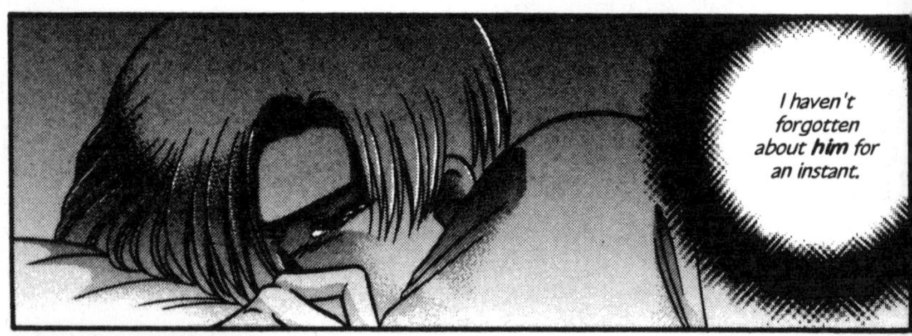
I haven't forgotten about **him** for an instant.

He's a liar.

Oh, good morning.
Though it's actually the afternoon.
Go wash your face and let's eat.
PEEL
Are you a maid or something?
PEEL
Very funny.
I'm cooking **today**, but as of tomorrow we'll take turns.

I took a look in the fridge. Doesn't look like you cook for yourself much.
Or do laundry.
So what if I don't? **Leave me alone!**
If you're not going to take care of yourself **now**, you can't complain **later.**
I am your bodyguard. Not your **mommy.** You understand?
LEAN
ぐぐ
That's...
Huh? Why are your eyes all red?
くいっ
PINCH
Have you been crying?
I didn't think you were that badly hurt.
~~~!!
ぐぬぬぬ
Get off a me!
Okay, okay, relax.
~~~

WHIRL

Now, go wash your face so we can eat.
PAT

SLAM
You're gonna break the door.

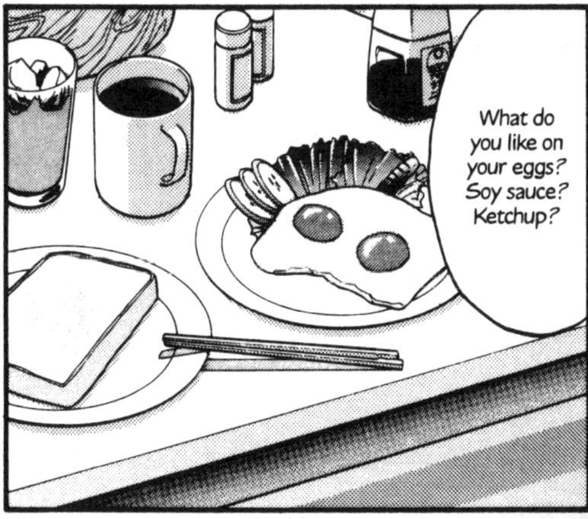
What do you like on your eggs? Soy sauce? Ketchup?

Worcest-ershire Sauce.
SIP
むすっ
Me, too!

If you put it on the yolk, then put the egg on the bread, it's really good! ♡
.....
MUNCH MUNCH
もく もく

Hey, how do you know Masa, anyway?

Sexual Relations.
SPIT
ぶっ

Just kidding. Did I get you?
You're **gay**!?
Yup.

D-Does Masa know?
Backing away
ささっ
Yeah, but don't worry. I'm not into **blondes**.

Do you...**like** Masa?
Hmm...
A little. I go for the stoic type.

An unrequited love, eh? Too bad.
Y'see, Masa's not gay.

He's not **totally** against men, you know.
I'll bet that's what frustrates you the most.
SMIRK
GULP

Hey, you'd better not make a pass at him!
Why not?
SMACK

My relationship with Araki has **nothing** to do with **you**.
HRNNNNN
SLURP

GRAB
ばっ
Hold it. You clean your own dishes.
You **can** do that much, right?
SHUDDER
ぴくぴくっ
And don't use too much detergent!
SCRUB
ガチャ
SCRUB
ガチャ
You shut up!!
He's so funny.
HEE HEE HEE
くっくっくっ
How can anyone who's in love with dreamy Masa be **such** a jerk!?

"He's not totally against men, you know?"

.....

Maybe I don't know Masa that well after all.

I knew he didn't like women all that much, but I never thought he might like guys.

Then again, he's around all yakuza men. Kyosuke's practically his wife.

He had a woman before, though. I don't even know her name.

FSHHH

Now that I think about it, we've never talked about this stuff.

SPLASH
I'm remembering strange things...
*There...was **that**, too.*

"Sorry. I got carried away with my joke."
Joke?

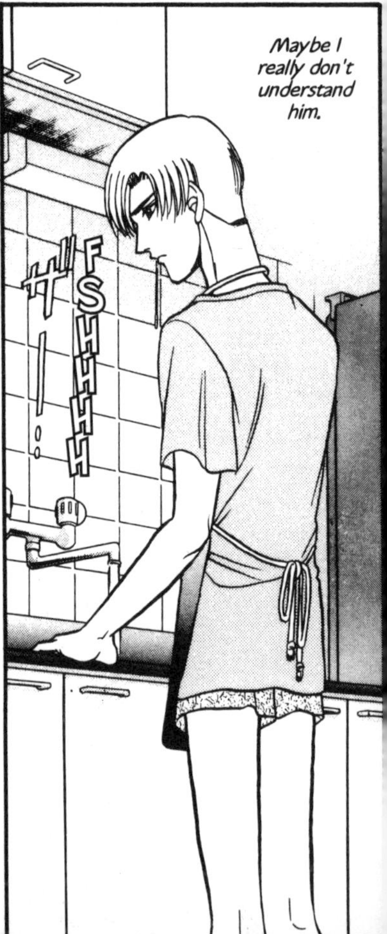
Maybe I really don't understand him.
FSHHHHHH

FSHHH

Tellya what: If you cheer up, then I'll sleep with you tonight.
I'm seriously going to kill you!!
PAT

23

You're late.
Sorry. We made a sale on our way out.

And you go wait inside, so you don't attract attention.
And go change your clothes. We're off to another job.
I know.

How long do I have to wear this disguise for?
Just wear it like you've been told! That getup is **safe.**

Maybe so...
Huh?

...But something's going on. I was chased tonight by some guy in Shinjuku.
Maybe he thought you were a hooker.
Heh Heh
Maybe.

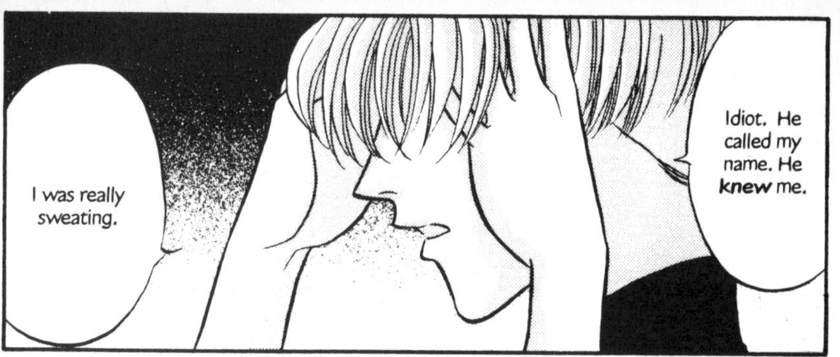
Idiot. He called my name. He **knew** me.
I was really sweating.

And the **real** Kai Sagano is in Tokyo, right? It'll be bad luck if we run into **him.**

Don't complain. You're just the figurehead.
We're the ones talking to the clients.
Yeah, **we're** the ones in danger.

Is everyone here?
Yes, boss.

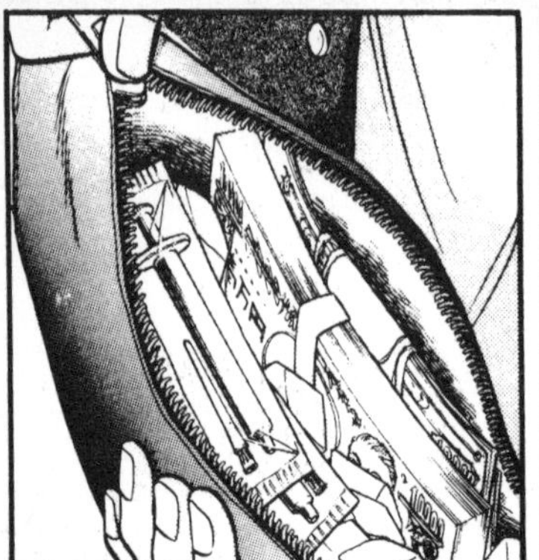

Here's the order. **And** your money. It's **all** there.
Okay.

It certainly is.

That means we'll make some **easy money** tonight.

I heard the"real" Kai got arrested last night.
Good news travels fast.

Heh...

WHAM

Gaak!
One of your victims... a blonde woman...was brought in, as well.

I **do** hope, for **your** sake, that you sufficiently covered your tracks.

She was hort! I was just tryin' to **scare** er a little, and...!

No excuses. If anything else falls short tonight, ***you'll*** be the one paying for it.

Maybe we can.
The Sagano family prides its **bloodline** above everything else.

Hold on a second.

Perhaps we could gather all their little soldiers together for a **funeral.**
Only...they won't realize that it'll be **their** funeral.

TOKYO INTERNATIONAL AIRPORT
新東京国際空港

Mr. J.B?

Yeah.

CLICK

I'll take you to the hotel.

A suite has already been reserved for you.

I don't need to rest. I'm here to **work.**

Mr. Tsuneya is dead. I want the photos from the crime scene. Can you **do** that, Mr...?

Koga.

Everything you've requested has been gathered. Negotiations are set to begin tonight, as scheduled.

Excellent.

Enjyoji! Wake up already!

すかー…
SNORE

すぅーっ
SNORE

.....

You might be able to get up if you didn't play video games all night! Now wake up!
YANK くいっ
Mmm...

Okay, I'm up.
もそもそ RUB RUB

ずりぽっ SWIPE

ばふっ POOMPH

......

Are you trying to kill me!?
PHAAAW
ぶはっ
Oh, good. You're awake.

You're really crazy, you know that?
YAWN
ふあ〜
Maybe you make me crazy.

Here, coffee. Drink up.
Thanks.

...gun-shots were fired...
PYUUN
ENN

...early this morning at an apartment complex in Tokyo's metropolitan area.
Eggs?
Yeah, over easy.

The whole world's going crazy.
Did you say something?
No, nothing.
Police have surrounded the building as the investigation continues…

The gunshots came from the apartment of a notable yakuza member.

Kai...
Hm?
That's Kai's building!
What ...!?

There are also reports of a shooting incident at the organization's main office in Osaka.

Police believe this may be a sign of **infighting** within the organization.

What's his number !?
BEEP
No casualties have been reported so far…

What's his phone number? We have to...
スッ
GRAB

Sagano must have been up to something.
What are you saying? Aren't you worried!?

We don't have to call.
Enjyoji !?

Isn't that rather cold of you?

There's nothing we can do about it.

He's your brother!
Half-brother. Besides, even if Kai were hurt I wouldn't be able to see him.
No sense worrying about it until we know for sure.

Don't we know that better than anyone?

I didn't want you--

--to see me like this!!

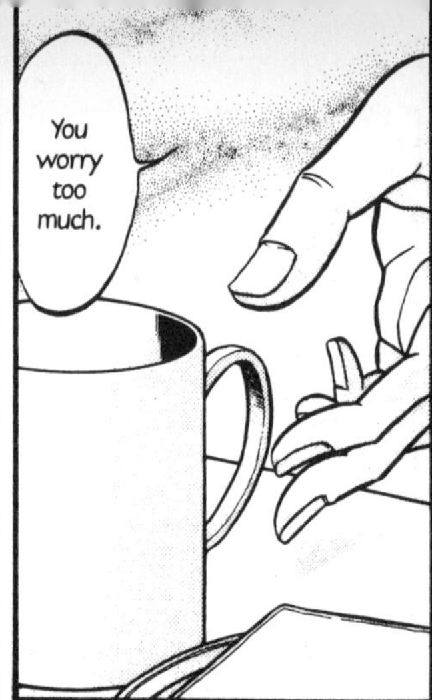
You worry too much.

I'll contact Araki later.
Don't worry about it, Ran.

But if I don't, **you** just take everything on yourself.
Huh? Do I?

Enjyoji.
Hm?

If you jump into anything dangerous without telling me, I'll never forgive you.

No matter what happens, you're ***still*** a member of the Sagano Family.
If something happens again...
Yeah.

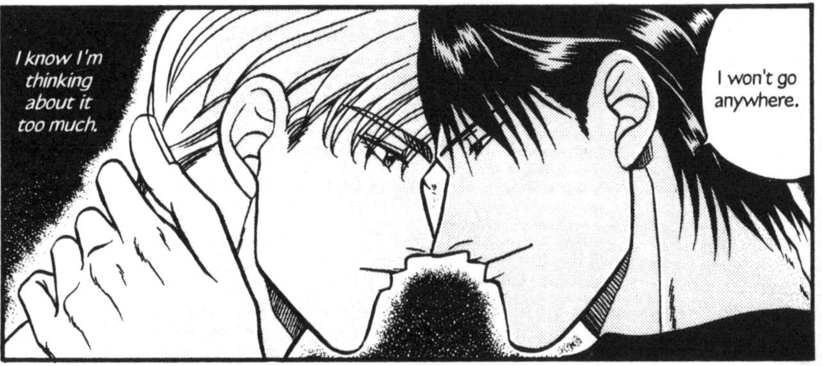

I won't go anywhere.
I know I'm thinking about it too much.

It's all right.

But I can't get rid of this anxiety.

If Enjyoji were targeted again...

How about taking a day off of work?
Sure, I could use a break.
Good. It's dangerous out there.

I'll lay off the late shift for a while.
Hmm... let's do it!
Wait a minute...
I'll stay home to keep you from worrying.

Wait! Hold **on** a second!
Why? What's wrong?

My eggs! They're ruined!
Damn it all
I give up.
I really do.

Mr. J.B. ...

...Here is the information you requested involving the incident with Mr. Tsuneya.

The cover story is that Mr. Tsuneya drunkenly drove his car into the ocean and drowned.

Unfortunately, the **autopsy** found several bullets in his skull. So far, the ever-efficient police have been **unable** to find the culprit.

I see.
Other than the ballistics report, there's no clue to the killer's identity...

...and I'm sure the murder weapon is **long gone.**

.....

Mr. J.B., we heard that you and Mr. Tsuneya had a little **trouble** before then.
Did he upset you in some way? Over **money**, perhaps?

Mr. Tsuneya wanted me to do a job. I **refused.**
There were **civilians** among the targets.

How noble of you.
WAVE

PSHT

FSSHT
Here are your targets.

The leader of Kansai's Shoryukai clan, **Takashi Sagano.**

And his vice-chief, **Masanori Araki.**

I'll also throw in a nice **bonus** if you find the man who killed Mr. Tsuneya... and you bring him to me alive.

You seek **revenge** for Mr. Tsuneya?

No. With these three gone, we will at last stand at the forefront.

In order for the new Tsuneya Family to advance, we need to chop a few **heads.**

Fine. But keep your team off the streets while I'm working.

May I ask why, Mr. J.B.?
It's simple, really. If your team acts, so will the police.

Fair enough. I'll withdraw my men.
Good.
Now, about the crime scene photos... Very hard to come by.

Japanese Police are coy.
They are desperate to cover up the murder because they have no leads.

I don't need them. I already know how Mr. Tsuneya was killed.
STAND

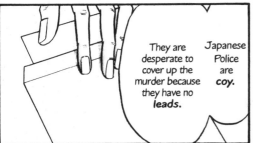

You sound like you know his **intentions**, too.
Was he a friend of yours?

There is only one man who could've fooled both the cops **and** the yakuza.

The man who taught me to speak Japanese...

...And the man I taught how to **kill.**

Kai's fine.
That apartment house was too dangerous, so we're at **my** place... Yeah.
How are things there?
The main office took three hits, Tashiro...
...but the family is fine.
DOI REAL ESTATE
土井不動
The place is **swarming** with cops.
OFF LIMITS
OFF LIMITS

In any case, lay low for a while.

We've got an idea of who's behind this...
...And it's probably because of that man, Tsuneya.

I'm sure you remember **him?**

You mean, the guy I...took for a ***swim?***
This is probably revenge for Tsuneya, yes.

Tsuneya's underlings have been spreading drugs around Tokyo using the Sagano name.

They're doing a fine job of dishonoring Sagano and **profiting** handsomely from it.

This is a **deep** grudge that's not going to end with a few gunshots.

Their next move will be to kill whoever did the hit on Tsuneya, and the ones that ordered it.

So you, your boss, and...**me**, huh?
Yes.
That's right.

We have to **get them** before the police do.
You're in great danger, but for now just look after Kai.
Yeah, I got it.
Anyway, you want to talk to him?
Ah, okay. See ya.
CLICK

Hmm.

I know you're mad. Just wait for all of this to blow over. Okay?
What did Masa say?

The headquarters was shot at, but the family's okay.
And Masa?
He's fine, too.

Masa's in more danger than me! That was just a **warning**!

Shhh.

Next time they'll be targeting **him**!

Calm down. It's all right.

Masa should be the one hiding out!!

He's in danger!

Araki will be fine.

He has plenty of people around to protect him.

It's all right.

...Although
the hug's
not so bad,
either.
!!
How'd you
like a nice
sausage
lunch?

I know
you're
upset.
You
should eat
something.
Maybe
get some
rest.

Shut
up,
you
jerk!
JERK
ばっ
Hey,
that's not
polite.
TWITCH
わきわき
TWITCH

Well,
it's nice
to see
you're
feeling
better.
Although I'm
disappointed
that I can't
cuddle you until
you cheer up.
I don't
need
that!

Aw,
too
bad.
What
should I
cook?
My
virtue is
in more
danger
than my
life.

Oh yeah, keep this.

It's a **transmitter.** Keep it on you, for protection.

Stick it to the back of your neck or something.

......

Hey Bodyguard. Am I the **only** one you're protecting?

Even I can't look after more than one punk at a time.

Ranmaru might be in danger, too...

I'll have to call him later.

So Kai's all right, huh?
Yes. I'll have someone look after you and Mr. Samejima, too.
Hey, no thanks.
It's already arranged with your father.
Look... No offense Araki.
But we're trying to be **normal**, here.
If my dad is so worried about me that he's risking **personal involvement**, that really does make me the son of a yakuza boss.

For my roommate's sake…
I want to stay as **far** from the yakuza as possible.

I'm fine now, and I'm being careful.
Tell that to my dad. And tell him that I do appreciate the sentiment.

I understand. We'll do our best to keep you **out** of the picture.
Please be patient. And be **careful.**

If I see Kai wandering around I'll be sure to grab him.
Please do.

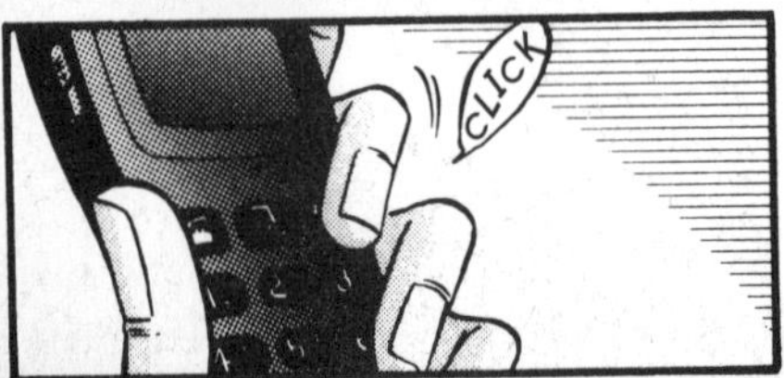
CLICK

I've gotta forget about the family... **and** that damn Kai.
Why was he being so suspicious in Shinjuku?
Enjyoji!

Are you done here?
Yeah. Did you talk to Mr. Araki?
I just finished.

Kai's moved out of his apartment and is staying with a bodyguard.
A body-guard?

Is he in **that** much danger?
It's all right! Nothing to worry about.

Let's go home.

Yeah... okay.
But there's still something worrying me.
As if there's a storm brewing, like before.

Oh yeah, I forgot to ask.
Hm?
When you came back from the dojo...

What did you want to talk about?

Well... I...

.....
I know you've got things to think about, right?
No rush.

Look, it's okay. Tell me when you feel like it.

Just let me know before you jump into anything.
Yeah. I will.

Your fingers look slimmer than before.
My fingers? I don't know, I didn't notice.

Hmm...
What?

Nothing
seems to be
wrong...

Does it
bother
you?

No.
Not at
all.

Hey, why are
you smiling?
What are you
thinking?
Just that
they're really
pretty.

Well, I'm going out shopping.

Stay here and sleep.
Yeah, yeah.

One "yeah" is enough!
What-ever!

SHUT
.....

ぱっ
POUNCE

RING
G-CHAK
Hello...?

Kai!? Thank God, I was worried!
Really? I'm glad.

I'm totally okay, though!
Is the idiot there?

Oh, **working?** Can you give him a message?
Tell him that the next time he's around Shinjuku or Shibuya...

...That someone's been selling drugs using **my name.**

It gets **better.** He wears a disguise to look like me, too. Tell Kei to stay clear if he sees the disguised "me."

No, I won't be leaving here for a while. If he sees me on the street, it's the **imposter.**

I'd rather go out and catch the guy myself...

...But the police and Masa told me to stay inside.

I under-stand.

I'll give you my cell number, just in case.

Okay. I'll call you if anything happens.
Oh, and Kai?

Both Enjyoji and I hope you're okay. Don't forget that.

.....

...Thanks.

.....
CLICK

I tell myself not to worry about it.
But I have this strange premonition.

Come home soon, Enjyoji.

There you are, Mr. Enjyoji.

Your order is here.

Yeah. Wow, look at it.
Can I get a case?
Certainly.

Huh?

The mood is very important.

I need a good plan.

He's supposed to be hiding out!
That **idiot**!!

Kai!!

GRAB

Stop sneaking around!
YANK

Why are you running, you idiot!?
THUD
CLATTER
Eeek!

"Eeek ...?"
TURN

FLOP

What the hell is going on!?

WHAKK

Huh?

These are...

The drug traders...
...The ones who are impersonating Kai!

THUD
ドサ

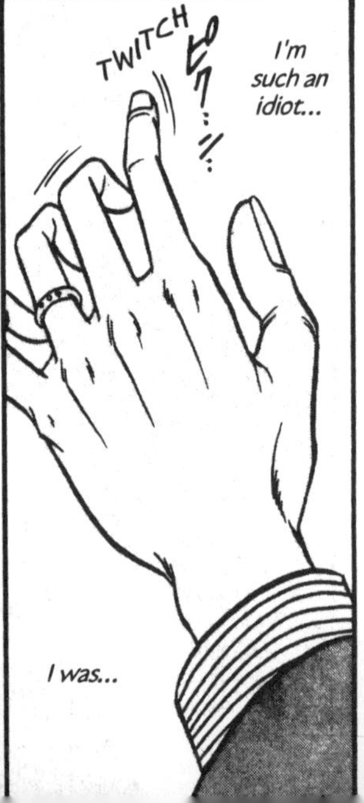
I'm such an idiot...
TWITCH
ピク…!!
I was...

...Going to give him the ring today...

Come
home soon,
Enjyoji...
It's too
dangerous
out there.
Kizuna IV // END

Afterthoughts

HEH HEH HEH HEH
うふふふふ
Finally, another volume of *Kizuna.* I'm sure there are many **unhappy** people.
I'm very sorry.
Facemask conceals identity.
It feels good, because her face is scary.
I know this series is **longer** than usual, so please be patient.

After this volume's cliffhanger, I got letters begging me not to kill Enjyoji! Come on! If **he** died, the story would be **over**!
Ooh, I feel better.
べろん
PLOOOP
Everyone's hearts would be racing.
It's a good thing that I got Ranmaru and Kei's rings out of the way.

I wanted to draw the ring scene in a very **dramatic** way.
My long hair makes me look like Tashiro.
I was worried if I'd be able to pull it off.
Don't compare me to you.

Oh yeah, look for *Kizuna* products from Animate, coming soon.
Don't forget the *Your All Volume 2* drama CD!
Good stuff, all around!*

*Note: These products are only available in Japan.

I just came back from Iidabashi Station, where I saw an advertisement for Biblos's *Kizuna* and *FAKE.*
I was so scared that I could hardly **look** at it!

FAKE is cool, but not completely homo, unlike Kizuna. I was so embarrassed.

Now all the commuters can enjoy our beautiful stars of *Kizuna!*

Ms. Kodaka, what kind of relationship do J.B. and Tashiro share?
ふら〜〜
FLOAT
Uh oh, here comes my chest-hair-loving manager, **Iwa**!
You haven't drawn chest hair in a while.

Their relationship is **profes-sional.**
No, they're lovers, right?

It's a **secret** !!
Which means you're secretly thinking of a way to **do** it, right~?
How trouble-some...

See you next time, for *Kizuna - Bonds of Love Volume 5!*

I'm so irresponsible...

About Kazuma Kodaka

I was born November 19th, 1969, in Kobe City and currently live in Saitama Perfecture. My blood type is O. Since volume three, Kei and Ran have been getting increasingly elaborate outfits. By the final volume, they'll be heaped in gold... (Kidding, kidding).

Interview with Kazuma Kodaka

During a recent visit to New York City to celebrate the release of *Kizuna: Bonds of Love*, Ms. Kazuma Kodaka made a rare public appearance at the Rockefeller Center Kinokuniya Bookstore to meet her fans and autograph copies of her best-selling Yaoi manga. During of our exclusive interview with Ms. Kodaka, the acclaimed author discusses the thrill of being published in America, how Yaoi has influenced her career, and much more.

BE BEAUTIFUL: How does it feel to finally have Kizuna: Bonds of Love *published in America?*

KAZUMA KODAKA: I was somewhat unruffled because other language versions had already been published in various countries. Some versions are strictly censored, even to the degree that the main love scenes have been deleted. Fortunately, the Be Beautiful version is less censored than any other versions, and I really appreciated it. Authors do not like censorship.

BE BEAUTIFUL: How does it feel to see American women embracing your books, as well as Yaoi manga in general?

KODAKA: It feels as if there is no border for the women who love Yaoi!

BE BEAUTIFUL: How has Yaoi manga influenced your career?

KODAKA: If I had kept drawing regular comics without stepping into this genre, my life would have been quite different. I changed my style completely, and I have now been drawing Yaoi manga quite a long time,

while being encouraged by many readers. Now I am invited all the way to New York. It feels like something unbelievable is happening. All in all, I owe a lot of my career to Yaoi.

BE BEAUTIFUL: What issues do you face as a female manga creator?

KODAKA: I don't face any particular problem. As a matter of fact, I had many more problems when I was drawing Shonen manga. I drew serial stories in weekly comics like *Shonen Champion*. Most of my works were "Gang" comics or "Hard Boiled" ones. Readers did not like female artists to draw those genres of comics. So, I was forced to lie about my gender at that magazine, crediting myself as a male artist for two years. Even if the secret would not leak out, I felt guilty to be lying. Now that everything is out in the open I have a great load off my mind.

BE BEAUTIFUL: Is Yaoi manga created predominantly by female authors because only females can understand and appreciate female sensibilities?

KODAKA: I think that women authors are just naturally more able to understand and create what women readers really want. The president of Biblos (Editor's note: The Japanese publisher for *Kizuna*) is not a woman, but the chief editor and sub-chief editor are both women. The president made the right decision in leaving everything to the women, I think, because the "You like to read this and so do I" style really works in Yaoi. You never fail in this way

-Continues in *Kizuna: Bonds of Love 5.*

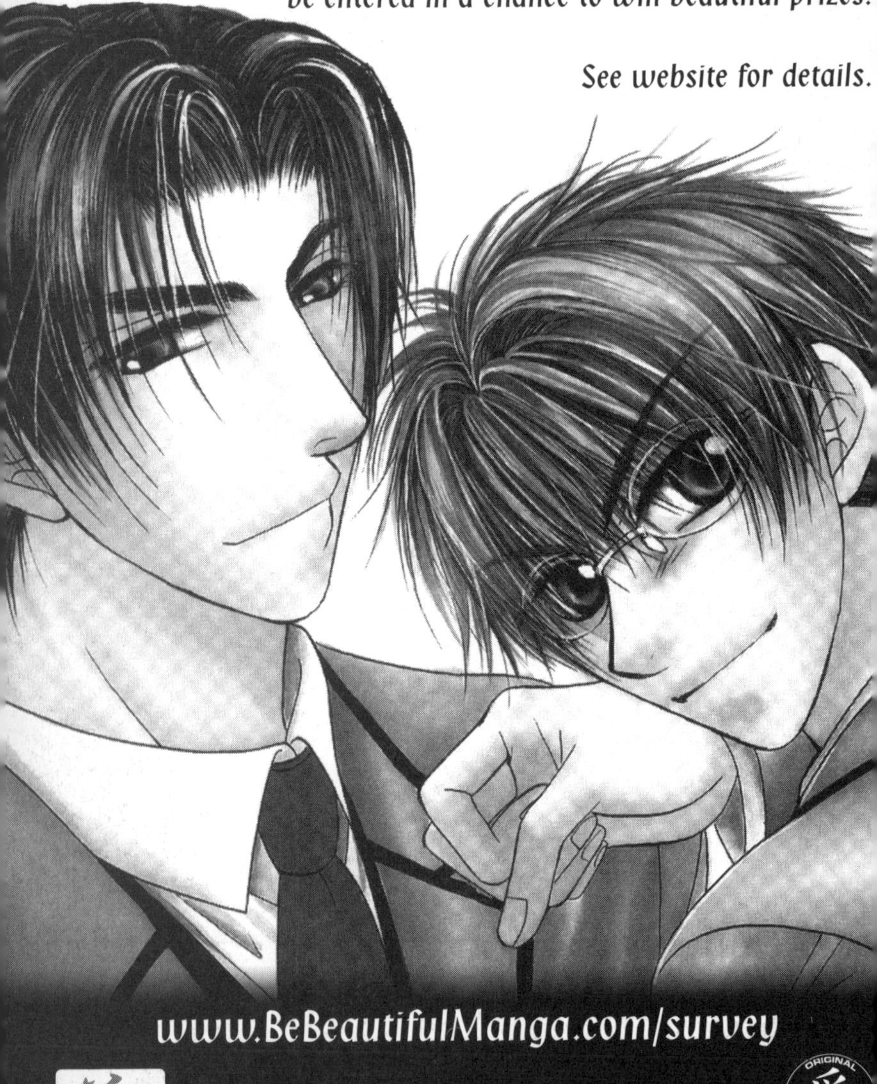

What
re you
nking!?
n on the
phone!

This sign reads "Tomare" and it means:

STOP!

THIS IS THE LAST PAGE OF THE BOOK! DON'T RUIN THE ENDING FOR YOURSELF.
This book is printed in the original Japanese format, which means that it reads from right to left (example on right).

Oh it's
nothing,
randpa.
Really.

You'll find that all Be Beautiful books that are part of our Original Yaoi line are published in this format. The original artwork and sound effects are presented just like they were in Japan so you can enjoy the comic the way the creators intended.

This format was chosen by YOU, the fans. We conducted a survey and found that the overwhelming majority of fans prefer their manga in this format.

Well
you...you
kinda...
busy.

The ideogram in the Be Beautiful logo is pronounced as "Be" in Japanese. It means "beauty" or "aestheticism".

The ideogram in the Original Yaoi logo is pronounced as "Ai" in Japanese. It means "love".